*There is at least one mouse in every image in this book.
See if you can find all 27 (not including this one).

Max the Ghost website

Max The Ghost coloring book

Author Page on Amazon

Blue Aardvark Press

Max the Ghost
wants to find a friend

Text Copyright © 2023 Marshall Almeida. All rights reserved.
Cover art and illustrations Copyright © 2023 Marshall Almeida.
All rights reserved.

No part of this book may be reproduced in any form without
written permission from the author.
Visit the author's website at www.marshallalmeida.com or
contact the author at marshallalmeida@gmail.com

This is a work of fiction. Any characters, locations or events
portrayed in this story are a product of the author's imagination.
Any resemblance to real world people, places or events
is purely coincidental.

First Edition

ISBN 13: 979-8-9882926-0-9

Published by Blue Aardvark Press. For any questions about usage
please contact the publisher at blueaardvarkpress@gmail.com

*Special thank you to all my proof readers: Leticia Silva,
Sofia Almeida, Karina Almeida, Xing Gilbert, Sarah Jimenez,
Marina Bravo, Gary West and Bedilia Jimenez.

Check out www.maxtheghost.com for t-shirts, coloring books,
stickers, art, etc. and news about future Max the Ghost books.

This book is dedicated to my wife Leti. Her unwavering love and support and her generosity in giving me the time and space to create and to be myself, made this book possible.
And to my daughters, Sofia and Karina who inspire me every day.

Max was a quiet and shy little ghost.
He had always lived on his own.

One night he set out to find a new friend.
He was tired of being alone.

The big house nearby had lots of rooms.
It was the perfect place to begin.

Carefully Max climbed up the front steps.
Then he bravely walked right in.

Max searched for a friend in the library.
He saw an owl that looked pretty good.

He moved closer and waved hello.
But the owl was made out of wood.

In the bathroom Max saw a spider.
He greeted her with a smile and a wink.

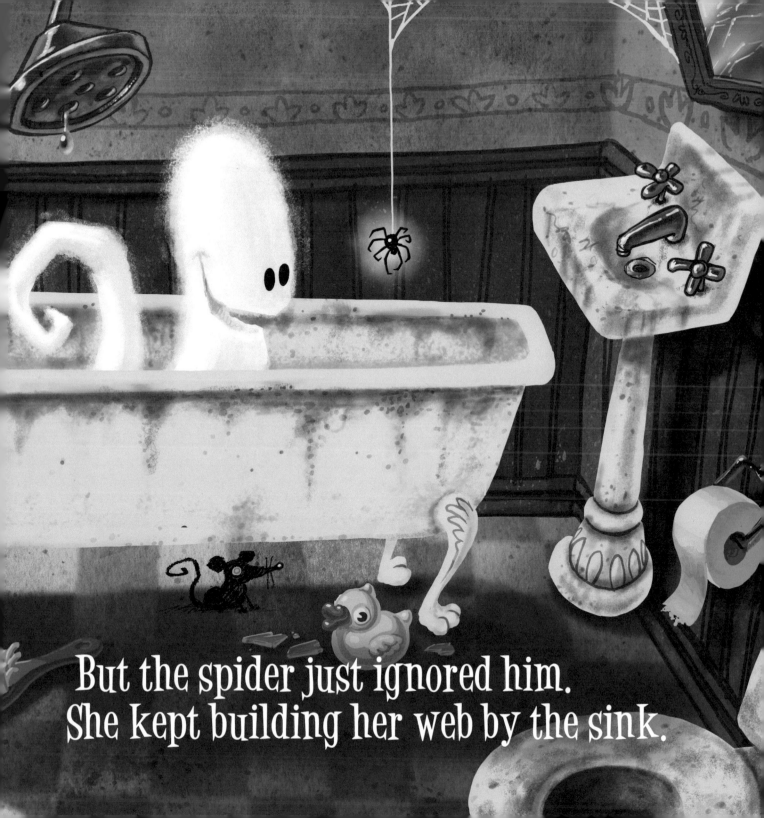

But the spider just ignored him.
She kept building her web by the sink.

He moved on to the big pipe organ.
It sat in the middle of the house. It felt
dusty and sad. Max played a few notes.
Then out popped a little gray mouse.

She shouted at Max. It was a loud, angry squeak. He had woken her up it seems. His organ playing spoiled her sleep. He ruined her sweet mousy dreams.

It was on to the playroom. Max grew excited. A smile stared back from in there.

But it was just an old rocking horse. It had a painted on smile and yellow yarn for hair.

In the kitchen Max found a long line of ants. They were marching across the floor.

The bugs were too busy. No time to make friends. Max continued right out the door.

In the basement he saw a silver trail.
He followed it all the way to the end.

There he found a little red snail.
He was too shy to be Max's friend.

Out in the garden he spotted a crow.
She was sipping from the bird bath of stone.

That crow saw the ghost and flew over the wall. Max was left sad and alone.

He heard a noise and peered in the greenhouse. Inside was a little brown mole.

The mole saw Max. He twitched his nose.
Then he scurried away down his hole.

He went down to the boat house for one last try. There he saw a sleeping black bat.

Max couldn't wake him. The bat snored away. He must be too tired for a chat.

Max felt it was time to stop for the night. He left the house on his own. He headed back home without a new friend. He would sit with the tombstones alone.

Then suddenly Max was frozen in place.
Something was holding him back.
When he turned around to see what it could be...

...Surprise! A little ghost dog named Jack!!

The little dog was not sure at first. Jack barked and licked Max on the face. That tickled. Max giggled and he ran down the hill. Jack quickly joined in the chase.

Soon they were skipping and having fun.
They played hopscotch and tag and pretend.
As the sun rose, they headed for home.
It was Max and his new best friend.

Now Max and Jack spend every night in endless games and fun. And so we say goodbye to them. Our story is finally done.

The End

For news about future Max the Ghost books, art and more,
check out www.maxtheghost.com

About the author:

Marshall Almeida lives and works in San Bruno, California, where he grew up. His studio is in the home that he shares with his wife, two daughters and a dog. As an artist and illustrator for more than 35 years, he has had many jobs, including making art for games, animated features, advertising and now children's books. You'll find more of his artwork at marshallalmeida.com or on instagram at instagram.com/marshallalmeida.

Made in United States
Troutdale, OR
10/29/2024

24232371R00024